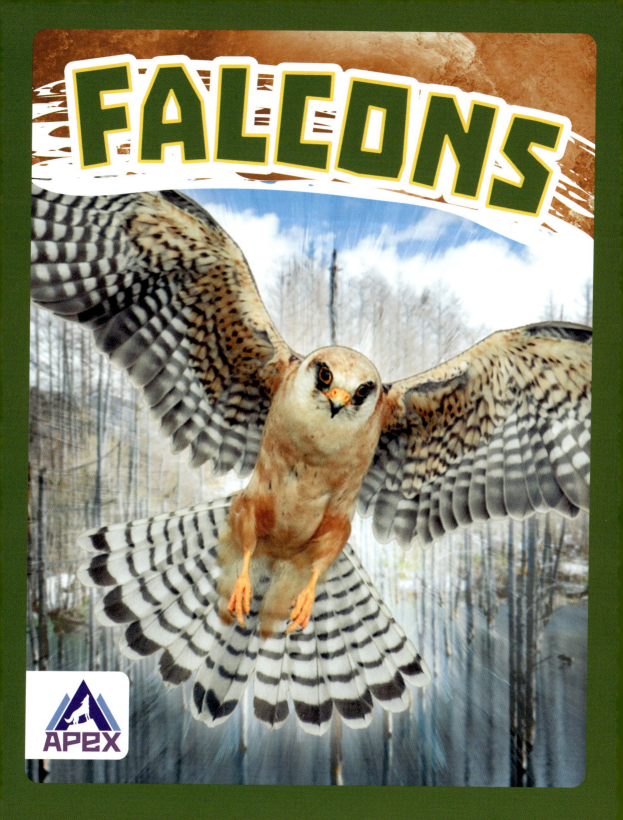

FALCONS

By Connor Stratton

WWW.APEXEDITIONS.COM

Copyright © 2022 by Apex Editions, Mendota Heights, MN 55120. All rights reserved. No part of this book may be reproduced or utilized in any form or by any means without written permission from the publisher.

Apex is distributed by North Star Editions:
sales@northstareditions.com | 888-417-0195

Produced for Apex by Red Line Editorial.

Photographs ©: Shutterstock Images, cover (bird), 1 (bird), 4–5, 6–7, 8, 9, 10–11, 12–13, 14, 15, 16–17, 18, 19, 20–21, 22–23, 24–25, 26, 27, 29; Unsplash, cover (background), 1 (background)

Library of Congress Control Number: 2021915653

ISBN
978-1-63738-142-7 (hardcover)
978-1-63738-178-6 (paperback)
978-1-63738-249-3 (ebook pdf)
978-1-63738-214-1 (hosted ebook)

Printed in the United States of America
Mankato, MN
012022

NOTE TO PARENTS AND EDUCATORS

Apex books are designed to build literacy skills in striving readers. Exciting, high-interest content attracts and holds readers' attention. The text is carefully leveled to allow students to achieve success quickly. Additional features, such as bolded glossary words for difficult terms, help build comprehension.

TABLE OF CONTENTS

CHAPTER 1
DIVING FOR PREY 5

CHAPTER 2
LIFE IN THE WILD 11

CHAPTER 3
FLYING FAST 17

CHAPTER 4
HOW FALCONS HUNT 23

Comprehension Questions • 28

Glossary • 30

To Learn More • 31

About the Author • 31

Index • 32

CHAPTER 1

DIVING FOR PREY

A peregrine falcon flies high in the air. It looks around the forest below. It spots a group of small birds.

Peregrines are some of the most common falcons on Earth. They live near water, deserts, and even cities.

The falcon dives toward the birds. It folds its wings close to its body. This body shape helps the falcon gain speed. Soon, it hurtles as fast as a high-speed train.

A diving peregrine falcon can go more than 200 miles per hour (322 km/h).

A falcon's fast dive is called a stoop.

The falcon opens its wings when it nears the ground. It slows down. Then it grabs its **prey**.

Peregrine falcons often catch and eat pigeons, ducks, and small birds.

Hunting with trained birds is called falconry.

HUNTING HELPERS

Falcons have helped humans hunt for thousands of years. People often train peregrine falcons. The birds learn to hunt and bring back prey.

CHAPTER 2

LIFE IN THE WILD

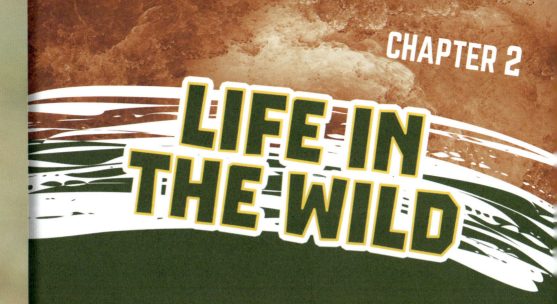

Falcons can be found almost everywhere on Earth. For example, some falcons live in the **Arctic**. Others live in forests or deserts.

Red-necked falcons live in grasslands and dry, open areas.

11

Some peregrine falcons fly 15,500 miles (25,000 km) in one year.

Some falcons stay in the same areas all year. But many falcons **migrate**. They fly to warmer places during winter.

Amur falcons fly from eastern Asia to southern Africa each year.

Female falcons lay eggs in nests. Chicks hatch from the eggs. Both parents bring food to the chicks. Later, young falcons learn to fly and hunt. Then they go live on their own.

Falcon chicks are born with soft, fluffy feathers called down.

Many falcon nests are in holes in trees. Others are on ledges of cliffs.

NEST THIEVES

African pygmy falcons do not make their own nests. Instead, they find the nests of other birds. They lay eggs there. Some even guard the nests from **predators**.

CHAPTER 3

FLYING FAST

A falcon's wings are long and pointed. Their shape is curved. Their feathers are **stiff**. These traits help falcons fly fast. The birds can move easily through the air.

Falcons use their long tail feathers to steer and turn as they fly.

Gyrfalcons can fly more than 50 miles per hour (80 km/h).

The gyrfalcon is the largest kind of falcon.

A falcon's **wingspan** can be more than 4 feet (1 m) long. And its body can be as long as 24 inches (61 cm).

Black-thighed falconets often give one another leaves as gifts.

TINY FALCONS

Several **species** of small falcons are known as falconets. The tiniest falconets live in Southeast Asia. They can be just 5.5 inches (14 cm) long.

Falcons also have strong hearts. Their hearts help them flap their wings fast.

A peregrine falcon's heart can beat up to 900 times in one minute.

Lanner falcons can fly very quickly to chase prey.

CHAPTER 4

HOW FALCONS HUNT

Some falcons eat almost anything. They are not picky. Other falcons mainly eat certain animals. For example, laughing falcons eat snakes.

Falcons often catch and eat other birds.

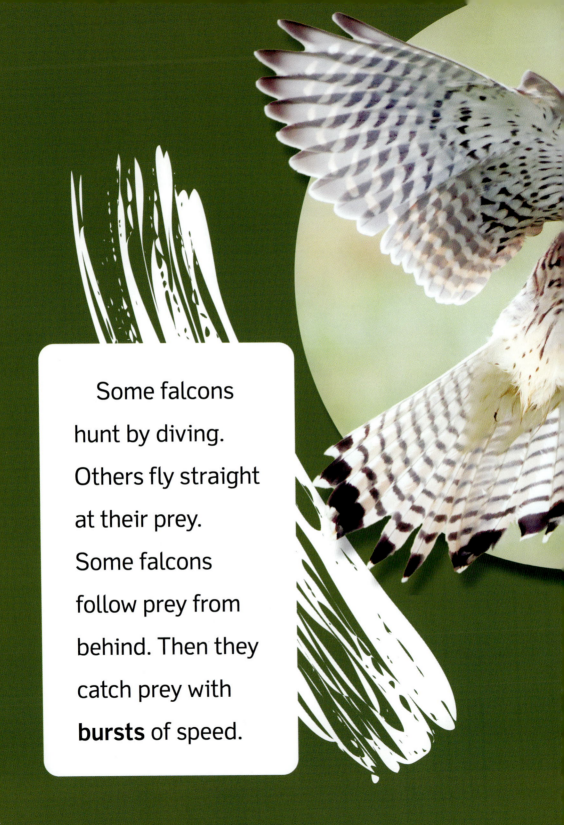

Some falcons hunt by diving. Others fly straight at their prey. Some falcons follow prey from behind. Then they catch prey with **bursts** of speed.

Kestrels are small falcons that fly above fields to hunt.

HOVERING HUNTERS

Kestrels are known for how they hunt. These falcons **hover** in the air. They watch for prey on the ground below.

A falcon's long toes help it grip prey with its feet as it flies.

Falcons catch prey with their feet. They use their sharp **talons**. Many birds kill with their feet. But a falcon uses its beak. The beak has a tooth-like hook. The hook can cut an animal's spine.

Some falcons can catch two birds at one time.

A falcon's hooked beak curves down into a sharp point.

COMPREHENSION QUESTIONS

Write your answers on a separate piece of paper.

1. Write a sentence telling one reason falcons are able to fly fast.

2. Would you want to learn to hunt with falcons? Why or why not?

3. What is the largest kind of falcon?
- **A.** gyrfalcon
- **B.** peregrine falcon
- **C.** falconet

4. Why would a falcon dive faster if it pulled in its wings?
- **A.** Folded-up wings use more energy.
- **B.** Folded-up wings can flap faster.
- **C.** Folded-up wings won't be slowed by air.

5. What does **hurtles** mean in this book?

*This body shape helps the falcon gain speed. Soon, it **hurtles** as fast as a high-speed train.*

    A. eats food
    B. moves very fast
    C. slows to a stop

6. What does **traits** mean in this book?

*Their shape is curved. Their feathers are stiff. These **traits** help falcons fly fast.*

    A. stories that are not true
    B. facts about a person's thoughts
    C. details about an animal's body

Answer key on page 32.

GLOSSARY

Arctic
An area in the far northern part of planet Earth that is very cold.

bursts
Short, sudden increases.

hover
To stay flying in the air in one spot.

migrate
To move from one part of the world to another.

predators
Animals that hunt and eat other animals.

prey
An animal that is hunted and eaten by another animal.

species
Groups of animals or plants that are similar and can breed with one another.

stiff
Not easy to bend.

talons
Long, sharp claws that birds use to hunt.

wingspan
The length from the tip of one wing to the other.

TO LEARN MORE

BOOKS

Hamilton, S. L. *Falcons*. Minneapolis: Abdo Publishing, 2018.

Mattern, Joanne. *Super Speed*. South Egremont, MA: Red Chair Press, 2019.

Sommer, Nathan. *Falcons*. Minneapolis: Bellwether Media, 2019.

ONLINE RESOURCES

Visit **www.apexeditions.com** to find links and resources related to this title.

ABOUT THE AUTHOR

Connor Stratton writes and edits nonfiction children's books. He loves observing birds wherever he goes.

INDEX

A
African pygmy falcons, 15

B
beak, 26

D
deserts, 11
diving, 6, 24

E
eggs, 14–15

F
falconets, 19
feathers, 17
forests, 5, 11

H
hunting, 9, 14, 24–25

K
kestrels, 25

L
laughing falcons, 23

M
migrating, 13

N
nests, 14–15

P
peregrine falcon, 5–6, 9, 12, 20
prey, 8–9, 24–26

T
talons, 26

W
wings, 6, 8, 17–18, 20

Answer Key:
1. Answers will vary; **2.** Answers will vary; **3.** A; **4.** C; **5.** B; **6.** C